BOOK
4

CAMOUFLAGE

CAMOUFLAGE

Bindi Irwin

with Chris Kunz

sourcebooks
jabberwocky

Published by Sourcebooks Jabberwocky, an imprint of Sourcebooks, Inc.
P.O. Box 4410, Naperville, Illinois 60567-4410
(630) 961-3900
Fax: (630) 961-2168
www.jabberwockykids.com

First published by Random House Australia in 2010.

Library of Congress Cataloging-in-Publication data is on file with the publisher.

Source of Production: Versa Press, East Peoria, IL, USA
Date of Production: April 2011
Run Number: 14965

Printed and bound in the United States of America.
VP 10 9 8 7 6 5 4 3 2 1

Dear Diary,

So what do you think of when I say Singapore? Maybe shopping, humidity, delicious Asian food, the night zoo? Well, on our recent trip to Singapore, we went to the opening of our wonderful friend Dr. Timothy Chan's new reptile park. It's on an island called Pulau Ubin, which, after the hustle and bustle of Singapore City, is like stepping into a different world. But things almost went horribly wrong when Saffron, Dr. Timothy's favorite Komodo dragon, went missing from her enclosure only a day before the reptile park was scheduled to open...

Let me tell you all about it!

Bindi

CHAPTER ONE

Bindi stared into the shop window, paying close attention to a gorgeous multicolored shoulder bag. "Check out that bag, Mum," she said enthusiastically. "It's so pretty!"

Robert wasn't too far away,

staring with undisguised admiration at a toy shop, which had boxes and boxes of remote-controlled dinosaurs just waiting to be bought.

"Mum, look at the velociraptor!" he said awestruck. "It looks so real."

Bindi was now peering closely at the price tag on the bag, looking worried. "Um, are Singapore dollars more or less than Australian dollars?"

Terri laughed. "Less." She glanced at the price tag. "But not that much less!" She dragged her kids away from the enormous shopping area that was part of Singapore's Changi Airport. "C'mon you two, ignore the shopping and let's head toward

4

the baggage claim. Dr. Timothy will be waiting for us."

Dr. Timothy Chan was an old friend of the Irwins'. He had worked as a reptile keeper at Australia Zoo for three years, and was now based back in his home country. In two days' time he'd be opening a brand new reptile park on the beautiful island of Pulau Ubin.

The Irwins had been invited by Dr. Timothy to attend the official opening of the park. So not only were they excited about seeing Dr. Timothy again, they were going to see a whole lot of reptiles, which was doubly exciting.

After grabbing their luggage, the Irwins went through to the arrivals area and, as promised, Dr. Timothy was there, a big smile on his face.

"Terri, Bindi, Robert! Welcome to Singapore!" He gave them all a hug. "You kids are getting bigger and stronger every time I see you. You'll be helping your mum catch crocodiles in no time."

Bindi was eager to set her friend straight. "We already do, Dr. Timothy."

Robert was not going to be left out. "Me too. Last time we went on a croc research trip, I helped too."

Dr. Timothy smiled. "Now why

doesn't that surprise me? Well, you kids will come in very handy at the Pulau Ubin Reptile Park," he said. "We've got a few crocs, a few goannas, three sailfin lizards, four different species of frogs, salamanders, rainforest dragons, and of course, we have—"

"Komodo dragons!" Bindi and Robert finished his sentence for him.

The Komodo dragon was Dr. Timothy's favorite reptile. The largest lizard in the world had been an obsession of his since he was a young boy. He had learned everything he could about the lizards, and was now one of the world's foremost authorities on the creature. No one knew more about Komodo dragons than Dr. Timothy!

"Well, let's get out of the airport. I thought I'd take you straight to the island so you can have a look around." Timothy looked at the Irwins, who were nodding enthusiastically. "Unless you're feeling tired, and I should take you to your hotel first?"

"No way! We want to see your reptiles!"

"I thought you might say that." He grinned. "Well, it's an interesting ride. I'll drive us to the ferry terminal, and from there we can take a bumboat over to the island."

Robert grinned from ear to ear. "Did you say bumboat?"

Timothy directed his guests out of the terminal and into the humid Singapore air of the parking lot. "Yes, a bumboat. They're traditional barges that have been used around the islands and on the Singapore River for hundreds of years. They're also called *tongkangs* or *twakows*."

Bindi couldn't let the joke end there. "Will we be traveling by bumcar, Dr. Timothy? Or bumcycle?"

Robert snorted with laughter, and Bindi dissolved into giggles.

Terri just looked at her kids. "Sorry, Timothy. My children are...

well, children, and any word with bum in it seems to be too darn funny for words."

He smiled at the kids, who were still doubled up with laughter. "Ah, I'm afraid this word is so familiar to me, I didn't realize it could also be funny." He considered it for a moment. "Yes, I guess it is sort of humorous."

He pointed in the direction of his car, and the four walked toward it.

"Here we are." Dr. Timothy grabbed their luggage and piled it into the trunk. Unlocking the doors, he gestured to the Irwins. "Your *bum*station-wagon awaits."

CHAPTER TWO

The ferry ride out to Pulau Ubin was short, but it was a refreshing journey after being cooped up in an airplane for so long. The scenery was beautiful. Dr. Timothy pointed out the pretty Changi coastal areas, and the coastline and mountainous regions of nearby Malaysia. The tranquillity was often interrupted by enormous jets flying overhead, but it all added to the excitement of the place. They were a world away from Australia Zoo, and it felt like an adventure was about to begin!

The ferry terminal was a hive of activity. There was another bumboat already docked, and couriers leaped on and off three smaller boats, unloading boxes and various equipment onto the wharf.

Dr. Timothy looked on, scratching his head in amazement. "I can't believe we're so close to opening.

I've been working toward this for so many years."

Terri smiled at her old friend. "And we're thrilled to be here to watch it happen, Timothy."

Timothy turned to the kids. "Are you ready for the tour?"

"You bet!" they chorused.

Timothy began to guide them toward the entrance gate, where workmen were putting the finishing touches to the admissions desk. "Okay then, I think we should start with the amphibian exhibit over—"

"Timmy, Timmy, come over here, darling," interrupted a woman's shrill voice.

Dr. Timothy visibly sagged at the sound. He pasted a smile on his face and turned to his guests. "Ah, I must introduce you to our esteemed patron."

"Well, well, this must be the famous Irwin family. How nice of you to visit our little island," said the small woman with the extremely large voice. She tottered over to them on her high heels. She wore an expensive-looking leather jacket and skirt, and her sleek black hair was scraped back in a tight bun.

"Terri, Bindi, Robert. May I introduce you to Mrs. Cynthia Yeoh."

The Irwins subconsciously moved away from Cynthia Yeoh rather than toward her. "G'day, Mrs. Yeoh." Bindi tried to be polite, but there was just something a little "ick" about the woman.

Terri put out her hand to shake Cynthia's, but Cynthia moved in and gave all three of them a hug. It was the most unwelcoming limp hug any of them had ever experienced. Her clothes were cold to the touch. It was almost like she was wearing...

"Ewww, are you wearing snakeskin?" Robert screwed up his face at the thought.

Cynthia let out a high-pitched

laugh. "Of course I am, darling boy. If I can't wear snakeskin at a reptile park, where can I wear it?" She laughed again.

The Irwins didn't share her sense of humor, and looked at Dr. Timothy, speechless.

He tried to smooth things over. "Cynthia has helped us raise funds and awareness for the reptile park," he explained. "Her husband, Mr. Jack Yeoh, is Minister of Planning and the Environment—"

"It's true, but everyone knows I do all the work around here!" Her shrill laugh filled the air again.

Robert couldn't help himself. He

put his hands over his ears. She would give a flock of galahs a headache!

Dr. Timothy continued. "Yes, she has been extremely helpful. And—"

"And tomorrow night I'm hosting *the* social highlight of the Singaporean calendar!" She gave a grand sweeping gesture, as if she was addressing a theater full of people.

"Oh, that's nice," Terri said. She turned to Dr. Timothy to ask him to begin the tour of the grounds, but Cynthia interrupted once more.

"It's for the opening of the park, of course, and there will be a traditional Chinese banquet at my home. A who's who of the Singaporean social scene will be there. My husband is away on business, but everyone else will be there. And media— there will be *tons* of media! You will be my guests of honor. I won't take no for an answer." Her head swiveled around as she caught sight of a passing employee. "Rupert," she screeched to him. "Get one of the boys to empty his boat. I need to get back to the mainland pronto!"

She tottered off toward the ferry with a dismissive wave to Timothy and the Irwins, who felt like they'd just been hit by a mini tornado.

CHAPTER THREE

Dr. Timothy turned to his guests. "Ah, I'm afraid I didn't get a chance to warn you about Mrs. Yeoh," he said sheepishly. His mobile phone rang. "Excuse me, I need to get this." He moved away from the others and started speaking quickly in Mandarin.

Terri tried to be tactful. "Well, I don't think I've ever met anyone quite like her before."

"Me neither," piped up Bindi.

"I hope I don't ever meet anyone like her again," added Robert.

"Robert, that's rude," scolded Terri.

"No it's not, Mum, it's truthful," replied Bindi on Robert's behalf. "She was wearing a snakeskin suit!"

Terri shuddered at the memory. "Yes, it was horrible. But don't say anything to Timothy about her. Anyway, it sounds like we'll be having dinner at her place tomorrow night."

"Do we have to?" Bindi asked.

"Yes, for Timothy. We're here to support him, and that dinner is obviously important."

Robert was shuffling his feet in the dirt. "When can we see the reptiles, Mum?"

"Look, why don't you and Bindi have a look around. I'll wait here for Timothy to finish his call and follow you."

"Okay, Mum."

The siblings looked at each other excitedly and raced off down the path.

"Let's go visit Dr. Timothy's favorite reptile," Bindi suggested.

They wandered down a dirt path toward a large enclosure, passing along the way a pair of Philippine sailfin lizards and a beautiful Fijian crested iguana. Next up was a large enclosure, where a regal-looking Komodo dragon was sunning herself on a large rock.

"There she is. That must be Saffron. Isn't she fantastic?!"

The kids knew that Dr. Timothy had been very lucky to get Saffron. Komodo dragons came from Komodo Island, in nearby Indonesia, but they were critically endangered. Dr. Timothy had plans to start a breeding program within the reptile park, and he hoped that in years to come, Saffron would produce offspring to help increase Komodo dragon numbers worldwide. So not only was she gorgeous, she was also vitally important to the success of Dr. Timothy's long-term plans for the reptile park.

Bindi looked admiringly at Saffron, who remained oblivious to the attention and raised her neck farther toward the sun. "I don't think I've seen a Komodo who's come straight from the wild before," she said. "She's definitely bigger than any female Komodo that I've seen before, don't you think?"

"Definitely. Nice long toes too," added Robert.

"She's drop-dead gorgeous," said Bindi.

Robert frowned. "I hope you don't mean her," he said, pointing farther along the path to where Mrs. Yeoh was having an animated conversation with a construction worker.

"Hmm, that's strange, isn't it?" said Bindi. "Wasn't she ordering someone around, telling them she needed to get back to the mainland 'pronto'?"

Just then, both adults glanced over in the kids' direction. Mrs. Yeoh looked annoyed to see them there and guided the worker away from the kids and out of sight.

Robert shrugged. "Maybe the boat wasn't clean enough and she's organizing a jumbo jet to pick her up instead."

Right on cue, a large aircraft flew overhead. He yelled over the engine noise, "See, told ya," but Bindi wasn't paying attention. She was frowning, staring after the departed adults. There was definitely something slippery about Mrs. Cynthia Yeoh.

CHAPTER FOUR

The Irwins woke early the next morning, very happy to have spent a relaxing night in a hotel bed. The kids were busy consulting the room service menu.

"Okay, so you can choose from

fresh fruit salad and yogurt, bacon and eggs—either poached, boiled, fried, or scrambled—or a basket of pastries with fresh juice..." Bindi looked up from the menu to see Robert frowning in concentration. "Or you can have—"

Robert's tummy growled. "What? There's more? But there are already too many choices. I want them all, and I'm so hungry I'm gonna have to eat the pillow if Mum doesn't come out of the bathroom soon!"

Bindi laughed. "Mmm, I don't think I feel like pillow this morning. I think I'm more in the mood for—"

The phone rang, interrupting

her. She jumped on the bed to reach it. "Hello?" she answered. "Oh hi, Dr. Timothy. Yes, thanks. How are—oh, okay."

She frowned and went to the bathroom door. "Mu-um, Dr. Timothy's on the phone."

Terri came out a moment later, her hair wrapped in a towel.

Bindi covered the mouthpiece and whispered, "Dr. Timothy seems really upset about something."

Terri frowned and picked up the phone. "G'day, Timothy." The kids watched Terri's face go from relaxed to alarmed to incredulous. "But I can't believe it. Yes...safe and sound there yesterday. I know, the kids mentioned—" She nodded. "Yes, of course I understand." She shook her head. "I know, it's terrible, and only one day from opening." She paused a moment while Dr. Timothy continued. "Yes, we'll be there as soon as we can."

Terri hung up the phone, pulling the towel from her head distractedly.

"What's wrong, Mum?" asked Bindi.

"There's been an incident at the reptile park. We have to head out there now."

Both kids looked longingly at the breakfast menu.

"But, Mum?" Robert pleaded. "We've got time for breakfast first, don't we?" His tummy growled again, punctuating his request.

"Let's get something quick downstairs then," replied Terri. "Saffron the Komodo dragon's gone missing from her enclosure."

Bindi exclaimed, "Sheesh, that's no good. They're carnivorous and have poisonous saliva. You don't want them roaming free around the island."

Terri nodded. "Exactly. That's why we're going to help search for her." She grabbed her bag and hotel key card.

"Okay, Irwins. Moving out. We've got a Komodo to find!"

CHAPTER FIVE

The Irwins headed for the ferry wharf by taxi, where poor Dr. Timothy, who looked like he'd aged ten years in one night, was waiting for them.

Terri and the kids gave him a hug.

"Don't worry, Dr. Timothy,"

assured Bindi. "We'll help you find Saffron."

"Well, this isn't quite what I'd had planned for your visit, but I'm really pleased you're all here."

Terri and Robert had just jumped aboard the bumboat when a TV cameraman and journalist hurried over to Dr. Timothy, who was still with Bindi on the jetty.

"Oh no," Timothy muttered to himself. "Just what we don't need. Bad publicity."

The journalist stuck her microphone in Dr. Chan's face. "Dr. Chan, is it true? Even before the controversial Pulau Ubin Reptile

Park has opened, you have a dangerous creature running wild?"

Bindi realized Dr. Timothy needed her help. She moved over to the journalist and gave her a sweet smile. "G'day, that's a pretty necklace you're wearing."

The journalist touched her throat, pleased with the compliment. "Thank you. And you are—?" She stopped, taking a closer look at Bindi, before adding, "Are you Bindi Irwin, from Australia? The Crocodile Hunter's daughter?"

Bindi flashed the journalist another smile. "That's right. And my family and I are here in Singapore because we're just so excited about the opening of Dr. Timothy Chan's awesome reptile park."

The journalist turned to the cameraman. "Did you get that, Tan?"

The cameraman gave the okay signal and continued to focus his camera on Bindi. "So, Bindi Irwin, what do you think about reports of an escaped reptile?"

Bindi looked toward the camera. "Dr. Timothy is a complete professional, and there are always last minute things that need fixing before something as amazing as a new reptile park opens. Don't worry, Singapore. When you turn up for the opening of the Pulau Ubin Reptile Park tomorrow, you'll be in for a bonza day, guaranteed. See you there." She gave the camera the thumbs up and then turned to the journalist. "Sorry, but we need to get moving. Lots to do today. See ya."

Bindi and Dr. Timothy climbed onto the boat, and moments later, the ferry was steaming toward the island.

Dr. Timothy turned to Bindi, impressed. "Bindi Irwin, you were amazing! Thank you."

Bindi giggled. "No worries. It was fun!"

Robert came over and handed

her an apricot danish he'd dug out of his pocket. "I was gonna keep this for later, but you deserve it after that performance."

Bindi didn't hesitate. "Yum, thanks," she said as she bit into the danish with relish. With her mouth full, she added, "Now we just have to find Saffron."

CHAPTER SIX

Unfortunately for everyone, as they arrived on the island, Mrs. Cynthia Yeoh was already there with her claws out.

"This is a total disaster, Timothy, and I hold you completely responsible," she screeched.

Dr. Timothy sighed. "Good morning, Cynthia. Do you know why there was a TV camera waiting for us at the Changi terminal?"

Cynthia's hand immediately went to her perfectly coiffed hair. "Really, TV cameras? I may have mentioned I'd do a press conference—"

Dr. Timothy's forced patience was disappearing by the minute. "Cynthia, I don't think that's a good idea at all. Firstly, I am the director of the park, and if anyone's going to make a statement, it should be me, and secondly—"

"Well, frankly, I'm amazed you're trying to throw your weight around

40

when you can't even look after a few cold-blooded creatures. The large lizard's disappearance is a disaster, and I'm sure it's been caused by that last-minute construction work you insisted happen in the python enclosure!"

"That reinforced fencing was necessary for safety reasons!" Dr. Timothy said exasperated.

Cynthia was now shouting. "The fact is, our star attraction is missing and you better comb every inch of this island and find it fast before our sponsors take their money and disappear too!"

Dr. Timothy looked defeated. "Yes, of course."

Mrs. Yeoh looked momentarily triumphant and then turned to the Irwins, who'd been watching the whole encounter.

She smiled sweetly at them. "I'm so looking forward to seeing you at the gala dinner this evening. I doubt that Timothy"—she gestured dismissively in his direction—"will be able to come now, but don't worry, I'll make sure you're looked after. See you there at seven."

She tapped Robert on the nose and patted Bindi on the head and tottered off on her ridiculously high heels. If the whole thing hadn't been so awful, Terri might have laughed.

Her children looked like they were going to explode!

Five hours later, the Irwins and Dr. Timothy met up outside Saffron's empty enclosure. "We've looked everywhere, Dr. Timothy. Saffron just seems to have disappeared," Bindi said, wiping sweat from her brow. Singapore was even more humid than Queensland!

Robert was extremely disap-pointed. "I can always find reptiles,

Dr. Timothy. I know where a croc will be hiding out in a river, or where a blue tongue will be hiding in the garden. I was sure I'd find a lizard the size of Saffron on an island!" He shook his head, worried. "Maybe I've lost my touch."

Dr. Timothy patted him on the back. "I doubt it, Robert. I agree with you. It's like Saffron's just vanished into thin air. I could've sworn there was no way she could get out of her enclosure. Komodo dragons are arboreal when they're young. That means—"

"We know," piped up Bindi. "They live in trees, but once they're older they're mainly terrestrial, which means—"

"—they live on the land," finished Robert.

Terri smiled proudly at the kids.

"I think I might hire your kids as guides, Terri. They know more about reptiles than most adults, that's for sure!" He glanced at his watch. "You guys need to head back to your hotel and get ready for the gala dinner," he said.

Bindi and Robert turned to Terri, looking hopeful. "Shouldn't we stay here and help, Mum?"

Dr. Timothy answered. "I'll need you to be at the dinner on

my behalf. Especially if Bindi can distract the media as well as she did this morning."

Bindi voiced the question they were all reluctant to ask. "What will happen if Saffron doesn't turn up before the opening, Dr. Timothy?"

He sighed a large, exhausted sigh. "I don't know. I don't think we can open without Saffron, and although she has the sweetest nature, who knows what might happen if someone who doesn't know about Komodos runs into her?"

Terri tried to reassure him. "It won't come to that, Timothy. She'll turn up. I know it."

"Keep those positive thoughts coming. And enjoy the dinner. I'll stay here and keep searching."

Robert said under his breath to Bindi, "I'd rather run into a hungry Komodo than Mrs. Yeoh any day."

"Me too. Much less chance of getting attacked," added Bindi dryly.

CHAPTER SEVEN

Later that evening, the three Irwins made their way up a driveway toward an imposing house in the affluent area of Bukit Timah. Looking across the landscaped gardens, Robert remarked, "Wow, Mrs. Yeoh's garden is about the size of the whole reptile park!" He pointed out an area that had a man-made waterfall next to a large bronze sculpture of a lion.

Bindi heard the sound of someone singing. She walked a little way off the path and saw a small girl skipping along and picking flowers. The girl looked up at her, smiled, and passed her one of the flowers in her hand. "Hello. Here's a hibiscus. You can have it if you like."

Bindi smiled, took the flower, and put it behind her ear. "Does this look okay?" she asked the girl.

"Yes, it suits your dress."

"Well, thank you. My name's Bindi. What's yours?"

"Bindi? That's a funny name. My name's Jasmine Yeoh, and this is my aunt's garden!" the little girl stated proudly.

"Well, it's a beautiful garden, Jasmine Yeoh," Bindi said. "But are you okay all by yourself out here?"

Jasmine looked offended. "I know I look little, but I'm actually almost five years old and I decided to take a walk around the garden before I went to bed. And I have an important job to do. I'm picking flowers."

Robert sauntered over. "I bet this garden has some bonza lizards in it."

Jasmine smiled. "Oh, have you seen the lizard?"

"Not yet, but I'll look out for some on the way up to the house."

The little girl waved good-bye and skipped off farther into the garden.

"Come on, kids," Terri called to them from just outside the front door.

Robert and Bindi turned back to the house and stared up at it, trying to delay for as long as possible the long and unpleasant night that lay ahead.

CHAPTER EIGHT

The butler showed the three Irwins into the banquet hall. The walls were covered in fine art, and a row of waiting staff stood ready to serve drinks.

The butler bent down to the kids

and said, "My name's Karl. Let me know if there's anything you need, okay?" He gave them a quick wink before heading out of the hall.

As soon as Mrs. Yeoh spotted the Irwins, she called, "Over here, darlings."

Robert muttered under his breath. "If she calls me darling again, I'll find a frog and put it in her wine glass."

They made their way toward their host. She was wearing a purple silk dress with what looked like some sort of fur wrap. Another animal skin! The kids grimaced.

Completely oblivious, Mrs. Yeoh gestured around the room, gaudy rings glittering on each finger. "Welcome, welcome to my *humble* abode. Please feel free to introduce yourself to people. In this room we have the crème de la crème of society. There are photographers everywhere, so make sure you look your best at all times! You're very lucky to be here, darlings. Champagne?" She grabbed a glass from a passing waiter and handed it to Terri, ignoring the children completely.

"Um, do you have something that the kids could drink?" asked Terri.

But Cynthia had turned away and struck up an animated conversation with another guest, who looked like she had a peacock feather sticking out of the back of her head.

The butler magically appeared next to them with two cold glasses of apple juice. "I didn't think you'd enjoy the champagne," he joked. They smiled gratefully as they took their glasses.

"Thanks, Karl."

The Irwins looked around the room at the loud, wealthy people chattering away. They started heading toward a quiet area when the unsubtle tinkling of a glass made everyone turn toward the head table, where Cynthia now stood.

"Welcome, honored guests, to

my gala dinner to celebrate the opening of the Pulau Ubin Reptile Park. Tonight you will have the pleasure of a ten-course Chinese banquet, but first I'd like to tell you a bit about the work that has gone into opening the park. I've done most of it, of course." She let out her shrill laugh as cameras flashed, and some of her guests laughed along with her politely.

She continued speaking, and the kids realized she wasn't going to stop anytime soon. Bindi whispered to Robert, "Let's get out of here!"

He didn't need to be asked twice. They ducked down out of sight and headed toward the far door. The butler was welcoming a late guest, and helping the man take off a full-length leather coat.

"Be careful! This coat is worth a fortune! I designed it myself," snapped the man.

The butler's expression didn't change. "Yes, sir. Of course. I'll put it in the coatroom."

"Make sure Cynthia knows I've arrived. We have some important business to discuss this evening."

"Yes, sir, and what name should I give?"

"Claudio Roggoletto, the leather-ware designer, of course."

He strode into the room, leaving behind the bemused butler.

Bindi and Robert threw Karl a sympathetic glance before slipping out the door.

"Well, it's no surprise to find out Mrs. Yeoh's friends are as demanding as she is!" Bindi whispered to Robert.

Outside the room, gold-painted passages led in three separate directions. It felt almost like a maze. They could hear Mrs. Yeoh's voice echoing from the banquet hall. Now that they'd escaped the party, they weren't sure what to do next.

They started walking down the

corridor nearest to them when they heard a bloodcurdling scream.

CHAPTER NINE

The echo down the passage made it hard to figure out what direction the scream was coming from. The kids raced back the way they had come and nearly collided with Jasmine, the little girl they'd met in the garden earlier in the evening. She was cradling her hand, looking disorientated, and crying hard.

"Jasmine, are you hurt? What's wrong?" asked Bindi.

Jasmine howled, "She didn't like my flower, she didn't like my flower."

"Who didn't like your flower?" asked Robert.

"Th-the big lizard didn't like my flower. I tried to give it to her and she...she bit me!" She showed the siblings her hand. There were puncture marks, blood, and a definite swelling between her thumb and first finger.

"Oooh, bet that hurt," Robert said.

Jasmine responded by howling even louder.

Bindi threw her brother a disapproving look. "Jasmine, where's your mum? We need to get your bite looked at by an adult."

Jasmine looked up fearfully. "Mother's away. And Aunty Cynthia's looking after me—but don't tell her."

"Why not?" asked Bindi.

"Because she told me to stay away from the Magenta Garden. That's an extra special part of the garden. And she said I wasn't allowed to go in there, but I'd been near there earlier, and I saw the big lizard through the hedge. She looked lonely, and I thought she would like a flower...like yours." She pointed to the hibiscus Bindi still had behind her ear.

"Jasmine needs to see a doctor right away!" said Bindi to Robert. She had a feeling this was not a normal garden lizard!

From the hall came the sound of applause. Mrs. Yeoh must have finally finished her speech.

Jasmine sobbed. "I feel sore...and dizzy...and my head hurts. But don't tell Aunty Cynthia. Don't tell her."

Bindi grabbed hold of the little girl as she sank to the ground in a faint. She hoisted her into her arms and ran toward the hall entrance, with Robert right behind her. Karl the butler appeared in the doorway.

"Little Jasmine! What happened to her?" he said, looking alarmed.

"Please, you need to call an ambulance. I think Jasmine has been bitten by a Komodo dragon, and their saliva is poisonous. She needs to be given strong antibiotics immediately."

The butler looked dumbfounded. "A Komodo dragon? Where? That can't be..."

Robert nodded, having come to the same conclusion. "If we're right,

Jasmine may die unless you call an ambulance right now!"

Karl wasted no time. He grabbed the unconscious little girl and ran with her toward a nearby study, where he could call an ambulance.

The kids were left alone in the large corridor for a moment. "He'll make sure she gets help," Bindi said.

Robert cast a quick look back in the direction of the banquet hall and then glanced toward the front door. "Are you thinking what I'm thinking?" he asked, grabbing a flashlight from his pocket.

Bindi grinned. "Let's go lizard hunting!"

CHAPTER TEN

The kids raced out of the main entrance to the house. Most of the garden was floodlit, but there was an area to one side that looked more private. They instinctively headed in that direction and soon came upon a large hedge. Robert shone his flashlight over the area. They could both see a beautiful magenta bougainvillea plant draped along the top of the hedge.

"The Magenta Garden!" the kids said in unison.

"How would Jasmine have gotten in?" Bindi wondered aloud.

They walked the length of one side of the hedge. They found a gate, but it was tall and wooden, with a strong padlock attached.

The bougainvillea was covered in little spikes, so they were pretty sure Jasmine hadn't climbed over the top of the hedge. A little farther along Robert spotted a break in the hedge, where a small person could fit through. "Probably through here," he said as he moved toward it.

Bindi called out. "Be careful, Robert. Take a peek if you can and make sure there isn't a Komodo waiting for you on the other side!"

Robert nodded. He turned off the flashlight and crept slowly through the thick hedge. Bindi waited anxiously. A moment later he reappeared.

"Yep, there's definitely a Komodo in there, but it's too dark to tell for sure whether it's Saffron or not."

They were going to need some

help—preferably without Mrs. Yeoh noticing. The kids started to race back from the Magenta Garden.

"I just don't get it," panted Bindi as they ran. "If it *is* Saffron, and I reckon it probably is, why would Mrs. Yeoh steal a Komodo from the reptile park she's been helping to promote?"

She didn't get to consider the possibilities any further, because the beam of a strong flashlight crossed their path. A gruff voice called out, "Hey, who's there?"

It was a security guard from the front gate—and he was looking mean.

The kids screeched to a halt,

crouched low, and scrambled for cover, throwing themselves into a nearby clump of bushes. The flashlight's beam made another sweep of the area. "I heard you. This is private property, and you will be prosecuted..."

He was walking closer and closer to the bush that hid the kids. As they lay among the twigs and leaves, they tried to quiet their ragged breathing, desperately hoping they wouldn't be discovered...

CHAPTER ELEVEN

The siren of an ambulance and a
squeal of tires made all three jump
with fright.

The guard turned back to the
main gates, grunted in confusion,
and started running as he saw two
paramedics start up the path toward
the house.

"Yowzers, that was close!" Bindi whispered to Robert. Robert remained frozen to the spot, and only his mouth moved as he said, "I'm good at this, aren't I? I could be a chameleon. You can't see me, can you?"

Bindi couldn't help laughing. The two kids crawled out from the bushes and could see the guard was busy with the paramedics, so they went the long way around to avoid being seen.

From out of nowhere the kids felt a hand on each of their shoulders. They screamed.

"What are you doing out here?"

The kids turned, scared. Who was it this time?

"You scared the life out of us!" squealed Bindi.

It was Dr. Timothy!

"Spending all that time around reptiles has given me some pointers on how to sneak up on prey," replied Dr. Timothy, grinning.

Bindi turned to Robert. "If someone's going to win a prize for camouflage skills, little buddy, it's definitely going to be Dr. Timothy."

Robert nodded. He had to agree.

The smile disappeared from Dr. Timothy's face. "Before you ask, we

75

haven't found Saffron, so I'm here to announce that we're going to have to postpone the opening of the park." He looked devastated.

"Umm, first we've got something to show you," said Bindi.

Dr. Timothy looked unsure but the kids grabbed hold of his hands.

"It won't take long," said Robert, and the three of them headed back to the Magenta Garden.

Bindi pointed out the hole in the hedge. "Take a look in there, Dr. Timothy," she said grimly.

He really wasn't in the mood for games but thought it best to humor his guests. He pushed his way through the hedge and gasped. "My goodness, it's Saffron!"

The kids nodded to one another. Thought so!

Inside the Yeohs' mansion, mayhem had broken out. There were swarms of guests milling about looking concerned. The paramedics had Jasmine on a stretcher and were taking her straight to the hospital. Photographers were snapping pictures as Bindi and Robert waded through the crowds, looking for their mum.

Mrs. Yeoh was nowhere to be seen, but the kids passed by the gruff man who'd been rude to Karl earlier. He was chatting to a group of women, who seemed to hang on his every word.

"Yes, darlings, this season I will be introducing a brand new skin into my range. Crocodile and snake are so last season. This will wow the fashion world like nothing you've ever known before!"

"Please put me on the wait list for it right this instant, Claudio. I can hardly wait!"

"Sweetie, this is so exclusive there won't even *be* a wait list," he chortled.

All of a sudden Bindi figured out why Mrs. Yeoh would want to steal a Komodo dragon, and she felt sick to her stomach. She moved over to the designer and glared at him. He ignored her, so she stamped on his foot as hard as she could.

He squealed and hopped around, holding his foot. "Owwww!"

Bindi shouted at him, "I don't know how important you think you are, but if you think for an instant you will be able to kill a Komodo dragon just to make a stupid handbag…"

There were a few gasps from the surrounding guests. Terri had made her way over to Robert and was all ready to launch into a lecture about not disappearing during a gala dinner, when she heard Bindi's outburst and stopped, concerned.

The designer glanced around guiltily and saw the guests looking accusingly at him. "What? What's wrong with trying something new? It *is* fashion, after all."

"You're talking about a beautiful living creature that deserves to wear the skin she was born in. And she is an endangered reptile, which makes it illegal! What's more, this is supposed to be a dinner to celebrate the opening of a reptile park, which has been set up to protect these extraordinary creatures!" Bindi shook her head in disgust.

The designer realized the crowd had turned against him. "Look, I didn't even want to do it. It was Cynthia. She wanted a new handbag in a skin that no one else had so everyone would be jealous of her."

At that moment the police entered the building, holding on to a struggling Mrs. Yeoh, with Dr. Timothy following closely behind.

The policeman spoke to Karl.

"We caught her sneaking out the back door."

"How dare you treat me like this in my own home?" she howled. "I've done nothing wrong. When my husband hears about this..."

Camera flashes were going off constantly now, but Mrs. Yeoh seemed oblivious. She was livid. But she stopped short when she saw Claudio. "You keep your trap shut!" she hissed.

Robert couldn't help himself. "Too late. You can hold your press conference...from prison."

Glaring at Dr. Timothy as she was led away by the police, she screeched, "If you hadn't brought those meddlesome Irwins here, everything would have been fine!"

CHAPTER TWELVE

The sun shone early the next morning as the three Irwins scrambled off the bumboat and raced toward the entrance of the Pulau Ubin Reptile Park.

"Mum, I can't believe you forgot

to set the alarm," Bindi said as she raced ahead of her family.

Robert was trying to eat a bagel and run at the same time. "I can't believe we didn't get a chance to eat breakfast sitting down again!" he groaned as he followed his sister.

A huge crowd was gathered outside the entrance of the park, and Dr. Timothy was already there. A beautiful, big red ribbon had been placed across the width of the gates. When Dr. Timothy saw the Irwins arrive, his smile became even bigger.

"And now, without further ado, I would like to officially open the Pulau Ubin Reptile Park. And to cut the ribbon, I ask my special Australian friend, Bindi Irwin, to do the honors. Come on up, Bindi."

Bindi raced forward and gave Dr. Timothy a quick hug. An assistant passed her a pair of scissors, and she snipped the ruby-colored ribbon in half.

The crowd cheered, the gates opened, and the Singaporean public raced through the gates, thrilled to be visiting the country's newest tourist attraction.

At 5:30 that evening the gates closed and Timothy and the Irwins sank into their chairs in the park's office, exhausted.

"Well, today has been a total success, and I owe it all to Bindi and Robert!" said Timothy, feeling quite emotional.

Bindi shook her head. "No, that's not right, Dr. Timothy. You set up this amazing reptile park, and we were just here to enjoy it."

Robert added, "And find a stolen Komodo dragon…"

Terri added, "And make sure a woman who thought fashion was more important than wildlife got sent to prison."

"And save a little girl's life," Dr. Timothy said.

"Oh yeah, that too," grinned Bindi.

ANIMAL FACT FILE

THE KOMODO DRAGON

🐾 The Komodo dragon is the largest living land lizard.

🐾 They can grow to lengths of over 9 feet and weigh up to 220 pounds.

🐾 Their saliva contains poisonous bacteria which will disable prey. The bacteria will cause infection, and often wounded prey will die within 2 to 3 days.

- Komodo dragons can be found on the Indonesian islands of Komodo, Rintja, Padar, Flores, Gili, Mota, and Owadi Sami.

- They inhabit lowland areas and mainly open grasslands, although hatchlings will usually inhabit more forested areas and are primarily arboreal.

- Komodo dragons eat almost any kind of meat. They will scavenge for carrion or stalk animals ranging in size from small rodents to large water buffalo.

- Baby Komodo dragons feed mostly on small lizards or insects. They do most of their hunting in the late morning.

- In the wild, Komodo dragons are normally solitary animals.

Become a Wildlife Warrior!

Find out how at www.wildlifewarriors.org.au

Bindi says: "As a Wildlife Warrior, I want to see animal skins stay on animals."

The adventures continue in

A WHALE
OF A TIME

Turn the page for a sneak peek!

CHAPTER ONE

Caitlin and Andy Blake, twelve-year-old twins, were blindfolded in the backseat of the car. It was a winter's day in Queensland, but because it was Queensland, the sun was still shining and the weather was balmy. The car was traveling along a single lane highway, passing through beautiful Australian bushland. It was really very picturesque but, sadly, not if you were wearing a blindfold.

"How much longer now, Bindi?" asked Andy, who was trying to sneak a peek from the bottom of his blindfold. He was a gangly, dark-haired boy, whose legs and arms sprawled in every direction. His twin sister seemed much more contained. She was shorter, with blond hair and a natural confidence. They were like chalk and cheese.

Bindi was sitting in the front passenger's seat. She glanced over at her mum, Terri, who was driving.

Terri raised two of her fingers to indicate they were about two minutes away.

"Not long, Andy. Hey, and no peeking!"

Caitlin was outraged. "What? Can he see where we're going? That's not fair!" She whacked her brother on the arm.

"Owww, I can*not*. Keep your hair on!" Andy hit his sister back.

Terri glanced in the rearview mirror. "You two, be nice to each other. We're almost there."

A few moments later the car pulled into the parking lot at Mooloolaba Wharf.

Bindi consulted her watch. "Right on time, Mum. Nice work. Okay, you two, time to take off the blindfolds."

Caitlin and Andy pulled off the blindfolds and paused for a few seconds to adjust to the light. The twins lived in England but were visiting Australia with their parents, who were speaking at an environmental conference in Brisbane today. They were old family friends of the Irwins, and this was the first time the twins had been to Australia. Bindi had enthusiastically offered to spend the day showing the twins around.

Terri grinned as the kids piled out of the car. "Well, I have to get back to the zoo, so have a terrific time today, kids," she said from the driver's seat. "Bindi, remember that Derek will drop you back off at the zoo after—"

"Mum!" Bindi interrupted. "Don't spoil the surprise!"

"I was going to say after*ward*," replied Terri. She waved good-bye and drove off.

"So where are we exactly?" Caitlin asked, looking around and noticing that they were near the water's edge.

"At Mooloolaba Wharf," answered Bindi. "Just in time to jump aboard a boat to go—"

"Whale watching?" Andy finished her sentence, sounding concerned.

He was looking at an impressive catamaran moored at the wharf with the name *Steve's Whale One* emblazoned on the side.

"Good guess, Andy!" answered Bindi, not noticing his frown. "This is the time of year when humpback whales travel up the east coast to warmer waters where they can reproduce, and that catamaran over there is going to take us on a fantastic cruise—"

Again, Andy interrupted. "On the water?"

Caitlin giggled and gave him a sympathetic smile. "You better tell her, Andy."

Bindi looked confused. "Tell me what?"

Andy gave his twin a pointed look. "There's nothing to tell, Bindi."

Caitlin didn't agree. "Well, Andy isn't what you call 'robust' when he gets anywhere near a boat..."

Bindi didn't understand.

Caitlin was enjoying herself. "He's more bookish. You know, very good at languages, not so good with travel sickness."

Bindi felt terrible. "Oh, Andy, do you get seasick? I'm so sorry. I didn't realize. I thought a day out on the water—"

"Look, it's fine. I haven't been on

a boat for years. I've probably grown out of getting seasick anyway," suggested Andy optimistically.

"Are you sure?" Bindi asked. "We can do something else. Maybe go for a bushwalk instead?"

Andy glanced at his sister, who was trying to hide her smile, and replied firmly, "Bindi, I would love to go whale watching. We'll have a wonderful time, as long as the weather doesn't become...really stormy. Like a cyclone, for instance," he finished, looking smug.

Caitlin's eyes widened. "The weather forecast is fine for today, isn't it, Bindi? On the news back home we've heard about some of the"—she gulped—"cyclones that have pounded the Australian coastline."

"Not to mention the shark attacks, all the poisonous spiders and snakes…" added Andy.

"And the British tourists that g-get lost in the outback," finished Caitlin, now looking totally spooked.

Bindi glanced from one twin to the other. At first she thought they were joking—but both of them looked genuinely frightened! "Come on, you two, Australia's the best country in the world. It's not scary at all! Follow me." She headed off in the direction of the wharf.

The twins looked at each other a little nervously.

Andy said, "Remember, Bindi feeds crocodiles and cuddles up to pythons in her spare time. She has a completely different idea of 'scary' than us."

"Thanks, Andy. That makes me feel a whole lot better!" Caitlin grimaced as she hurried to catch up to their fearless Australian friend.